With love to Pamela and Albie,
who are sweeter than all the
chocolate in the world x ~ C.S.

For Sarahsaurus, Jay-Rex, and
Theosaurus Rex ~ N.O.

Published in the UK by Scholastic, 2023
1 London Bridge, London, SE1 9BA
Scholastic Ireland, 89E Lagan Road, Dublin Industrial Estate, Glasnevin, Dublin, D11 HP5F

SCHOLASTIC and associated logos are trademarks and/or registered trademarks of Scholastic Inc.

Text © Chae Strathie, 2023
Illustrations © Nicola O'Byrne, 2023

The right of Chae Strathie and Nicola O'Byrne to be identified as the author and illustrator of
this work has been asserted by them under the Copyright, Designs and Patents Act 1988.

ISBN 978 0702 31362 2

A CIP catalogue record for this book is available from the British Library.

Printed in China
Paper made from wood grown in sustainable forests and other controlled sources.

1 3 5 7 9 10 8 6 4 2

www.scholastic.co.uk

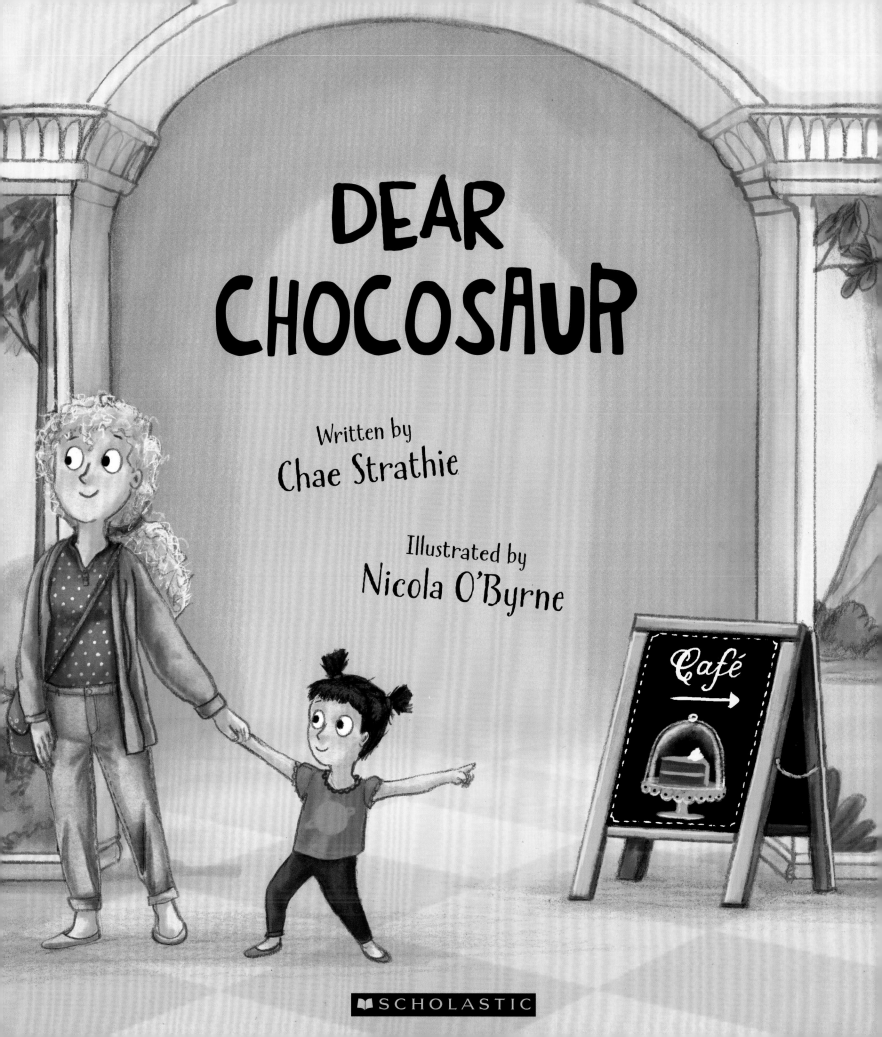

DEAR CHOCOSAUR

Written by
Chae Strathie

Illustrated by
Nicola O'Byrne

Café

SCHOLASTIC

Max was so excited.

Today was a museum day,
which meant today was a DINOSAUR day!

As soon as he and Mum and Dad and Millie had been to
the café for a snack of chocolate cakes and milk, he dashed
straight to the Dinosaur Hall to see his gigantic friend, T.Rex.

Dinosaur Dora was telling a group of visitors about what dinosaurs liked to eat.

"It's very interesting," she said. "Most of the dinosaurs were plant-eaters, which means they mostly ate leaves and twigs. Some even swallowed stones to help crush hard plants!"

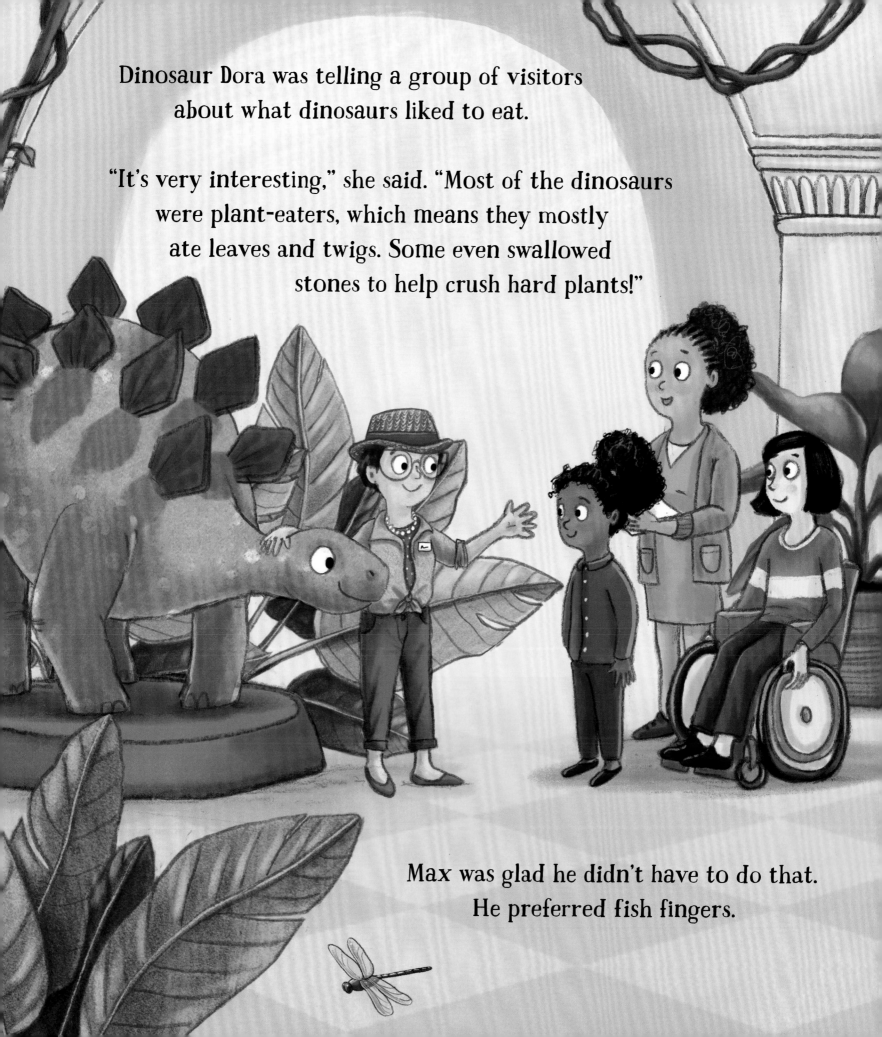

Max was glad he didn't have to do that. He preferred fish fingers.

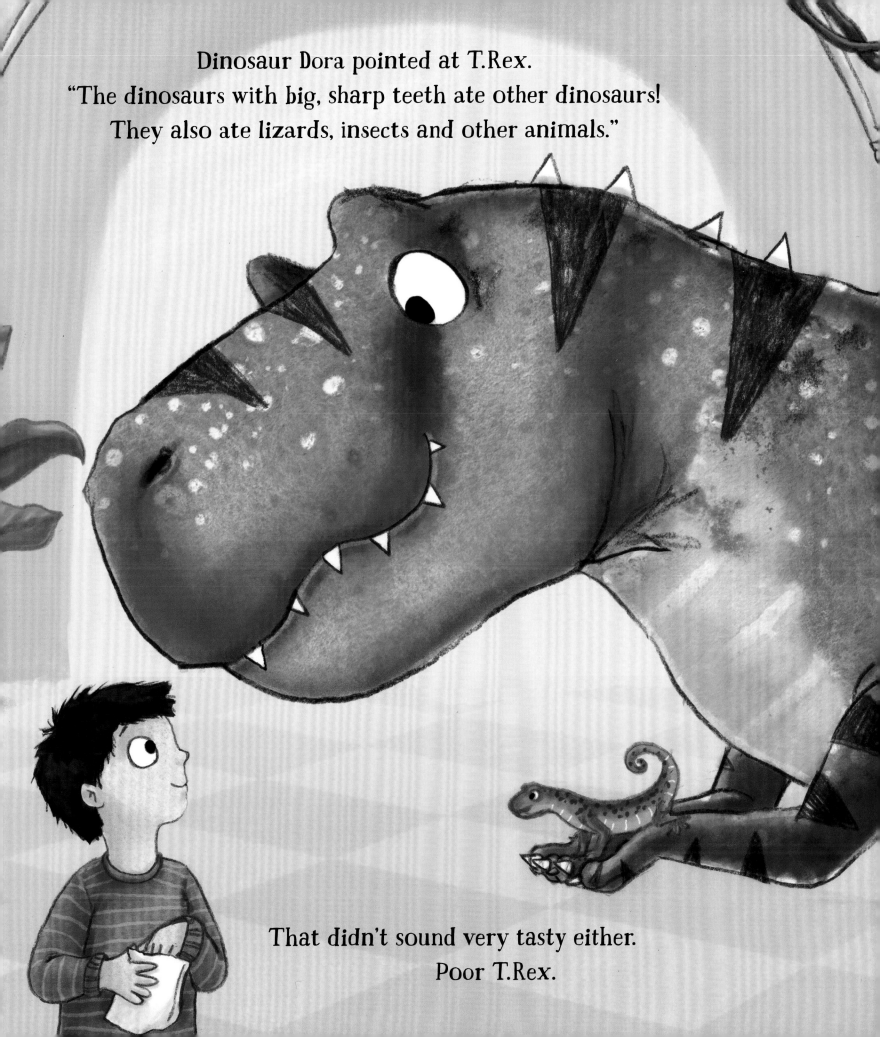

Dinosaur Dora pointed at T.Rex.
"The dinosaurs with big, sharp teeth ate other dinosaurs!
They also ate lizards, insects and other animals."

That didn't sound very tasty either.
Poor T.Rex.

When Max got home he couldn't stop thinking about the dinosaurs eating twigs, stones and . . . creepy-crawlies! EW!

So he decided to send T.Rex a present.

KEEP OUT

Dear T.Rex,

ROOOAAARRR!!! How are you?

I don't know if you saw me at the museum today — you were being very quiet and still, probably because you were listening to Dinosaur Dora's talk.

I was sad to find out that you never got any treats to eat, unless you count eating an Edmontosaurus as a treat.

I have put several chocolate buttons in the envelope so you and the other dinosaurs can try something yummy for a change. Have you ever eaten chocolate before? Chocolate is one of my favourite foods.

Yours sweetly,

Max

Usually Max had to wait quite a while for T.Rex to reply, but the very same day an email arrived.

Send **Attach** **Address** **Fonts** **Draft**

To: max@dinomail.com

Subject: More, More, Mmm-ROAR

Dear Max,

Oh. My. Days.

I can't believe what's happening in my mouth. I put those round brown things you sent in there and now it's all sweet and gooey and TOTALLY AMAZING!

Is this what chocolate is? If so I want MORE, MORE, Mmm-ROAR!

We definitely didn't have anything like this back in my day. 70 million years ago, sweet shops hadn't been invented yet. I ate stuff that I found lying around half-eaten – I didn't even chase other dinosaurs much, which is a bit embarrassing.

Anyway, I'm very interested in exploring this chocolate thing more, so if you can send me more, please do.

ROOOAAARRR!!!

T.Rex

Max didn't have any buttons left, but he knew Millie had a chocolate Easter bunny in her bedroom, so he sent that instead.

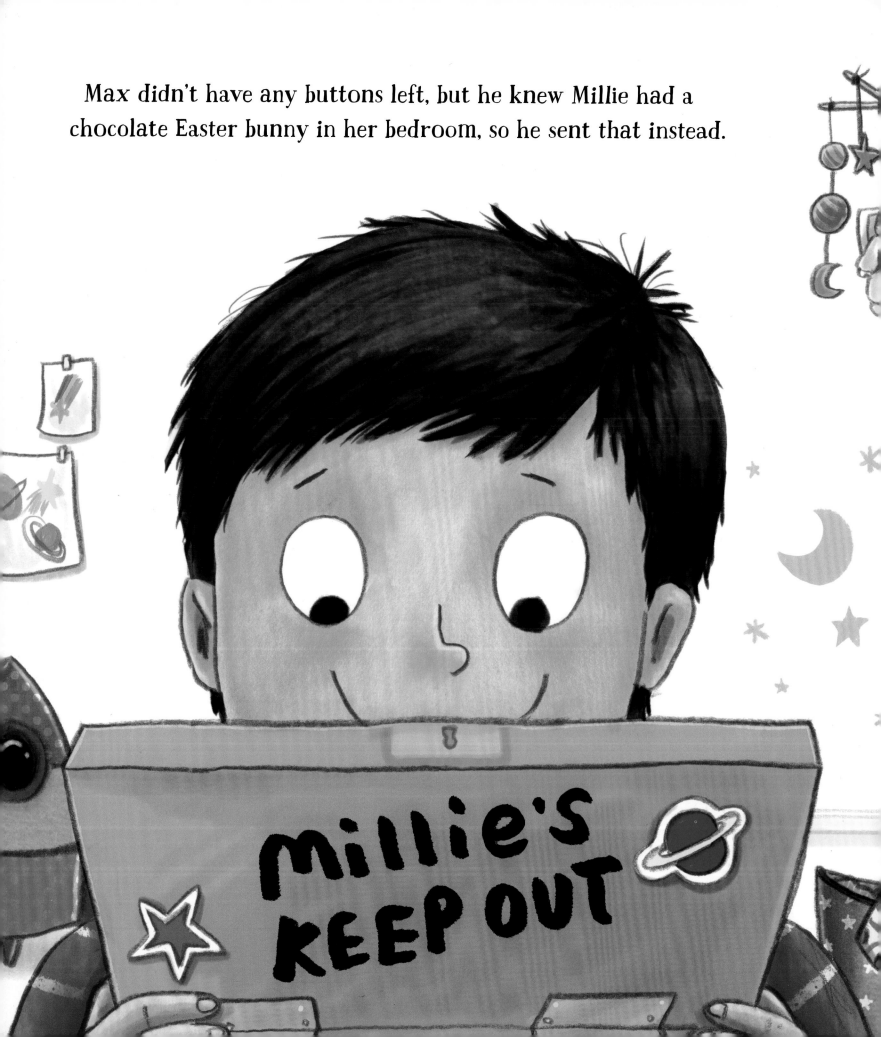

MiLLiE'S
KEEP OUT

Dear T.Rex,

I'm glad you liked the chocolate buttons.
Here's a small chocolate bunny for you to try.
I'm sure Millie won't mind you having it, even
though she was going to give it to Mum for Easter.

I think it will taste better than the stuff you found
lying around. That would be like me eating a sausage
I found under a hedge, which is pretty gross.

What did the other dinosaurs think of the chocolate
buttons? I bet little Nanosaurus went wild for
them, and Triceratops too. Don't forget to share
the rabbit as well!

Yours sharingly!

Max

It turned out Millie *did* mind
Max sending her Easter bunny
to some dinosaurs.
Millie was a fan of space,
not dinosaurs.

Max was helping tidy the garden, to make up for taking things without asking, when a letter arrived in a museum envelope.

CITY 🦖 MUSEUM

Dear Max,

WOW!

I had a dream last night that I was swimming in melted chocolate and there were lots of little chocolate bunnies splashing about. Then I drank all the chocolate and ate all the bunnies and then I woke up.

I definitely tried to share the chocolate with the other dinosaurs to ask them what they think about it, but it was just so good that I ate it all myself. Sorry. Please send more immediately.

ROOAAAARRRR!!

T.Rex

Max was not allowed to send any more chocolate to the dinosaurs.

But Dad made a suggestion...

Dear T.Rex,

I'm sorry but I can't send any more chocs and I have to remind you to brush your teeth very thoroughly. They are so big and shiny — as long as a ruler — and it would be a shame if they were damaged by eating too many sweets! I don't think a dentist would enjoy a visit from you.

Here is a recipe for a chocolate cake that I make with Dad. It's scrum-diddly-umptious! Maybe Dinosaur Dora can make it for your 71-millionth birthday! Don't forget to give the others a slice.

Yours cakily,

Max

A few days later, another email arrived.

But it wasn't from T.Rex ...

To: max@dinomail.com

Subject: Cake

Dear Max,

Hello. It is Triceratops here. And Nanosaurus. I'm here too.

We wanted to let you know that T.Rex made the cake from the recipe you sent. We found him in the museum kitchen and the place was a TOTAL mess!

He had an enormous chocolate cake right in front of him and we thought he was going to offer us a bit, but then he chomped the whole lot in ONE bite.

Then he became very red and admitted you'd sent chocolate buttons and a chocolate rabbit but he'd eaten them all himself and hadn't shared a single thing. We only managed to eat some of the chocolate frosting that he splattered all over the walls.

We thought you should know.

Roar and roar,
Triceratops and Nanosaurus

Max was shocked.

Later that day, he and his family went on a trip to the beach,
but he bought a postcard so he could write to T.Rex.

Dear T.Rex,

Well, well, well. What am I going to do with you?

I know chocolate is THE BEST, but SHARING it makes it taste better!

Millie and I had an Easter egg hunt at the beach and I gave her some of the chocolate I found. It made her so happy. And me too.

I shouldn't really do this, but here's a box of mini chocolate eggs and some Easter chicks. Remember to share!

Yours ice creamily,

Max

Mr T.Rex
The City Museum
Middle Street Square
Greenville
DN0 5AR

Max wondered if T.Rex had been keeping even more chocolate to himself.

He didn't have to wait long to find out.

Dear Max,

I am very embarrassed about keeping all the chocs to myself.

To make up for it I organised an Easter egg hunt all around the museum using the eggs and chicks you sent. We dressed up and searched in every room, and at the end I shared my basketful with Triceratops and Nanosaurus, and they said I was WONDERFUL!

Thank you for being such a good friend.

ROOAAAARRRR!!

T.Rex

The next week, Max was on a school trip to the museum.

Once they'd been to the Ancient History Hall and the Costume Hall, they went to the Dinosaur Hall.

Dinosaur Dora was there to give them a talk about fossils.

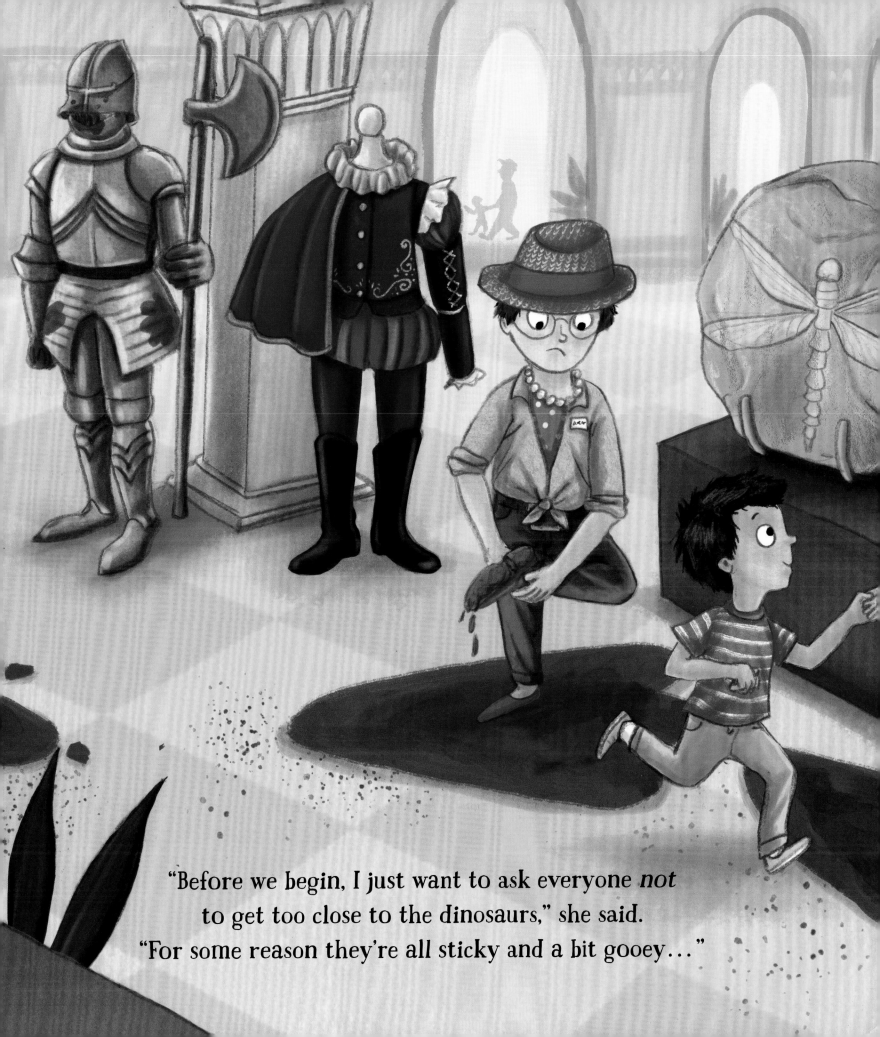

"Before we begin, I just want to ask everyone *not*
to get too close to the dinosaurs," she said.
"For some reason they're all sticky and a bit gooey..."

"...and they smell very strongly of CHOCOLATE!"

Dear Maxosaurus Rex,

Here's a little something I'd like to share with you.

Dinopals for ever!

ROOAAAARRRR!!

T. Rex